This book belongs to:

_____

A catalogue record for this book is available from the British Library

Published by Ladybird Books Ltd
80 Strand, London, WC2R 0RL
A Penguin Company

2 4 6 8 10 9 7 5 3 1
© LADYBIRD BOOKS LTD MMVIII
LADYBIRD and the device of a Ladybird are trademarks of Ladybird Books Ltd

ISBN: 978-1-84646-934-3

Printed in China

My best book about...

Me

Written by Mandy Ross
Illustrated by Kate and Liz Pope

This book is all about you –
from the top of your head,
to the tips of your toes!

Do you look a little bit like any of these children?

Can you point to all of these things on your own face?

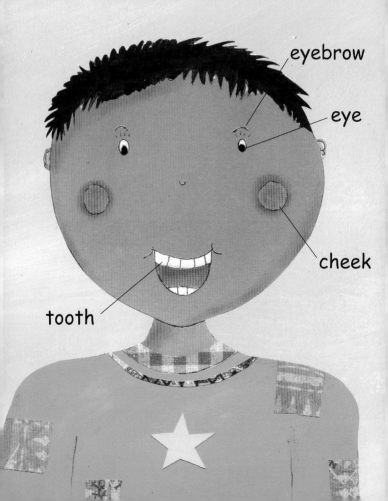

eyebrow

eye

cheek

tooth

Arms are good at waving, lifting and hugging.

Legs are good at running, jumping and dancing. Can you do any of these?

Fingers are useful for counting.
How many fingers have you got?

And how many toes?

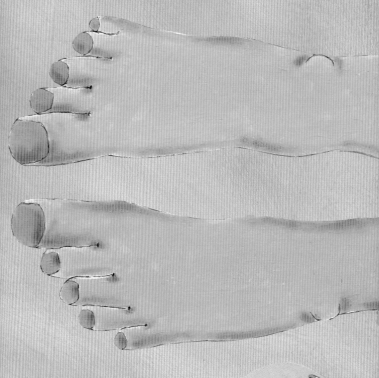

Fingers are good
for tickling toes!

Hair comes in lots of different colours and styles.

What does your hair look like?

Teeth help you to chew your food.
How many teeth have you got?

Can you pretend to brush them with your finger?

The bones inside your body help you to stand up straight and tall.

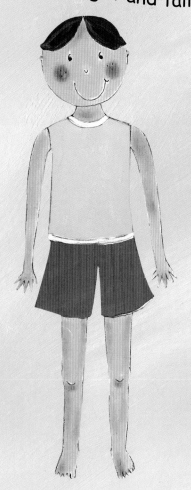

Can you feel your bones inside your skin?

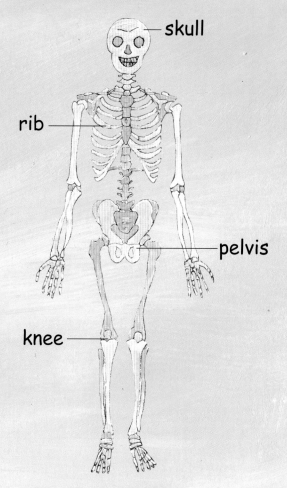

skull

rib

pelvis

knee

Skin does an important job.
It keeps the dirt out – and keeps
your blood in!

Clean knees

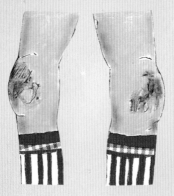

Dirty knees

How are your knees looking today?

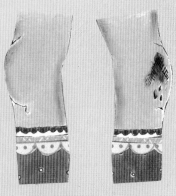

Oh dear!

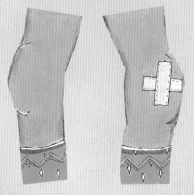

All better

We have five senses: we can look, hear, smell, taste and touch.
Can you tell which sense is which?

Your body needs all kinds of different things to eat and drink. Which of these do you like?

We have lots of different feelings.
Can you point to the happy face?

Can you point to the face that looks cross?

Busy bodies are healthy bodies!
Which of these do you like doing?

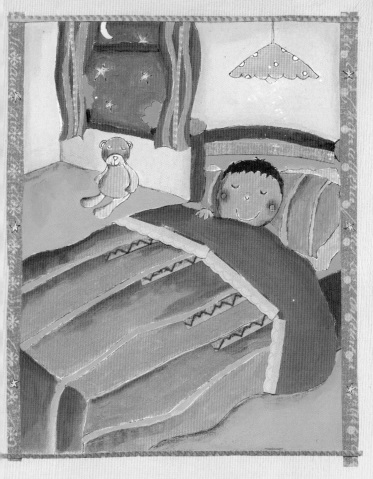

And healthy bodies need to rest, too.
Can you sing a lullaby?
Night, night!